MW00882997

The Case
of
Missing Max

Otakara Klettke

Illustrated by Minette Wasserman

ISBN 978-0-9979070-3-2

To my daughter Sofia and loyal pets that have been by my side my whole life.

You are my biggest inspiration.

As my thanks for buying this book I would love to give you another book by Gr. Acie:

"A DOG'S GUIDE TO HUMANS;
How to Pick and Train Your People"

For **free download** go to
http://bit.ly/dogsguide

Table of Contents

1. Meeting Bella 1

2. Dog Park 11

3. Mission: Find Max 19

4. Need to Explore 29

5. Alley 35

6. The Afternoon 41

7. Clock Is Ticking 45

8. Back in the Alley 51

9. The Scariest Moment of My Life 57

10. Cat Fight 67

11. Home Sweet Home 79

Dictionary 83

Sneak Peek of Detective Bella Unleashed

    Book 2 .... **85**

Acknowledgements **95**

About the Author **97**

1
Meeting Bella

My name is Gr. Acie. That is not Gracie. Gr. is a title I earned for being at the top of my class in Paw Paw School for dogs. It is a famous private school for upper-class dogs in the town where I used to live. Ever since I earned that title, my mom Kathleen started calling me Grrr. Acie and her human friends call me Gracie.

Kathleen is a good human mom and a pack leader. She is young for human years and quite pretty. The fur on her head is long and dark, and her voice is always loving. Even when she gets mad at me, she still uses a sweet voice when telling me not to get into trouble again.

Now Kathleen got this new job where she is a pack leader. She is very excited about that. She tells me that she is getting her own office in this new place.

We are moving to a new town to live in a new house. I wonder what life for a dog is going to be like there. Kathleen and I used to live in an apartment, but since I am a dog, Kathleen decided that it's best if I have a yard.

I sure do appreciate that. I love to play outside and inhale smells in the grass. Humans aren't fit for life outdoors. Some live their whole lives indoors using the outdoors only to transfer themselves into another indoor place. I am so happy Kathleen isn't like that. Well, she couldn't live outdoors. She lacks the fur and thick skin needed to do that, but she has the outdoor spirit. She likes to run with me and takes me to several parks.

That is all one lucky dog can ask of her human mom.

Today is a moving day. I love to travel with Mom. But today I am especially excited. Finally, our car stops in front of the new house. Kathleen opens her door, and I jump on her lap and then onto the driveway. I want to smell this place.

"Acie!" calls Kathleen after me. She is upset I didn't wait for her to get out first, but how could I with all the excitement trapped inside me. I run to the sidewalk.

"Don't do that! You could get run over," Kathleen exclaims, shaking one finger in the air. Her voice has that sweet and upset tone. I know she isn't really mad. She is just pretending to stand her ground.

Then she starts talking to the moving guys who have parked the big moving truck behind our car. The sun is warming up my fur and the air has the smell of late spring. I stand in front of a big house with a picket fence around it.

Before I have a chance to explore any-thing, I hear "woof, woof" coming from behind me. *Who is that?* I turn around. There is a dog pulling an older lady on the leash behind him. He is wagging his tail and choking at the same time, from pulling so hard on the leash.

I wait politely for him to get to me. We sniff noses.

"Are you new in this neighborhood?" he asks.

"Yes," I reply, "do you like it here?"

"It's okay. Just not as safe for a dog as it used to be," he says and starts to choke again as his owner pulls him away.

Arrrrrr. Why do people have no respect for our conversations? There may be something dangerous out there and I will never know because his human pulled him away.

The dog disappears out of my sight and I forget all about him. My life is about to be filled with exploring a new place. I am thrilled to check out this place on such a nice day.

The house is quite big for one human with a canine companion, but the best thing about it is the yard. It's not as big as a park, but it is outside. I get to have my own green lawn! My own territory!

I need to sign it right away! I walk inside while Kathleen is bringing a whole bunch of boxes into the house. She tells the moving guys where to take our bed and other furniture. Humans tend to do a lot of boring activities. I try to get Kathleen's attention, but she has no interest in joining me in the exploration of the best part of our property. No big deal. I can explore it for us both.

I discover that I have my own doggie door leading to the backyard! The porch feels spacious as soon as I step onto it. Mom is going to like it. I head straight for the three steps that lead down to the grass. The yard is a rectangular shape with a wooden fence. This is the way humans mark the edges of their territory. Most of the yard is covered by grass with a fruit tree in the middle and bushes along the side of the fence. There are birds chirping in the tree. *Too bad I can't catch them.* The bushes have flowers blooming on them. Something that humans like. I am interested in those bushes because they may provide a shelter for fun creatures that I could hunt.

I take a big whiff of air. *Aaaaaaah. This is going to be great.* My nose is taking in air like a birthday balloon. I detect something worth examining. I start sniffing the air with sharp short inhales and exhales.

That is the scent of another dog*! Am I going to have a canine neighbor?* I better watch out. I generally get along with the upper-class dogs. I am an educated purebred poodle. But some dogs just don't know how to behave. *This is going to be interesting.*

I go over to the fence and start sniffing. No peemail on the fence. That means the neighbor is a girl like me. At least I won't live next to a crying Romeo.

The neighbor's back door opens. I push my weight forward on my front paws like I do at beauty exhibitions, anxious to see her. *Who is she?*

But a human puppy wobbles out instead. It is a nice little toddler wearing nothing but a diaper. I push my ears back.

A moment later, a large blue-eyed dog comes out. A Siberian Husky. She grabs the human puppy by the diaper and gently pulls her in. Then she sticks her nose back outside and sniffs the air. She knows about me. She is good. Let's see if she will be a good neighbor.

"Hey, you at the fence. What are you doing there? You don't belong here," she barks at me while running toward the fence.

"I live here," I respond with the medium alert in my voice. I am not sure if this is a friendly meeting yet.

"No, you don't."

"Yes, I do. We just moved here with my mom."

The dog behind the fence sizes me up. I am not used to that. I retreat a little. I guess neither one of us is sure about the other.

"What's your name?" she asks.

"Gr. Acie," I reply, not sure if giving my title is a good idea.

"Grrracie? Odd name."

"No, it's Gr. Acie," I correct her. "I earned the title Gr. Don't you know it?" I say, a bit disappointed. I was hoping she would have a little more class.

"Not really. My name is Bella," she says and wags her tail.

So, she is friendly. Maybe not so educated, but friendly.

"Who are your humans?" Bella asks.

"Kathleen is my mom. It's just the two of us," I respond politely.

"Now that explains why you have some fancy title from some fancy canine school." Bella laughs. "I have five humans. Mom and Dad, and they have three puppies. The oldest boy Kyle is thirteen, Sofia is going to be ten, and Lucy is almost two and still not potty trained. I was already living with my family when Lucy was born."

Then, I hear the most familiar voice in my life. "Acie! Come on in!"

"That's my mom. I better run! Smell you later!" I bark and run toward Kathleen at the back door.

2
Dog Park

"Wake up, Mom!" I am standing on top of Kathleen, wagging my tail. That's one of the few cues humans understand. "We gotta' check out the dog park today!"

I am not too fond of the way she smells. I want to lick off that cream she puts on her skin, but Kathleen isn't usually too pleased with that idea. So, I stick to wagging my tail. Hopefully she will get that I have a much better sense of smell one day; I understand what smells good. In all honesty, humans have terrible taste when it comes to smells.

It is the first morning in our new home. The house looks funny with all the boxes around. I jump off Kathleen and run to the kitchen to get a drink. It is fun to run between those boxes. It's like being in a maze.

In the kitchen, my bowls for food and water are on the floor. As soon as my tongue touches water, I can't stop drinking. While I'm drinking I roll my eyes around to examine the room.

The kitchen looks almost moved in, but most of the countertops are covered with boxes that contain things to go in those cupboards. The kitchen table and chairs are already in place.

I loved our old kitchen because it always smelled like food. This one is still missing that smell but I know it won't take long before Kathleen changes the aroma of this place.

I like that my mom cooks. She is good at sharing her food too. I do have to sit still and look very intently at her; otherwise she would forget to give me some of her food.

We have three bedrooms, which is more than enough according to Mom. We are going to turn one of them into an exercise room. I am not too sure what Mom means by that; the room isn't that big to set up an agility course, but I am willing to give it a shot.

There are two human bathrooms. These places are a total mystery to me. I don't get humans and their bathrooms. Besides those, we have a laundry room with a canine torture area. When Kathleen first saw it, she exclaimed: "Look, Grrrr. Acie, we have a utility sink! You have your own bathtub with a showerhead!"

Seriously?

I return to the bedroom where Kathleen is still sleeping like a dog after a ten-mile hike. I jump back up, stomp my paws on her chest, and lick her face with my freshly watered tongue.

"Good morning Gr. Acie. Aren't you excited?" yawns Kathleen.

An hour later, we are finally on our way to the dog park. Humans take forever to get out the door. Kathleen does all kinds of grooming on herself every single morning and night. She uses all sorts of things to get herself clean. It's super weird.

When we finally get to the dog park, Kathleen unclips my leash and calls out, "There you go. Have fun Acie!"

Then I run and run. I love bouncing my paws on the spring grass. Several dogs come over and smell me. That's the downside of coming to the park for the first time. Finally, I stop while those dogs sniff the air by my tail.

"Give her some space," orders a familiar voice.

"Bella?" I look up in surprise.

"What? Do you think only dogs with fancy educations come to the dog park?" Bella laughs.

"No, of course not. I just didn't expect to run into someone I know," I reply apologetically.

"My mom takes me here almost every day after Dad goes to work and Kyle and Sofia go to school. Lucy and I get to run here," she explains. "C'mon, let me introduce you to a few nice dogs."

Some dogs offer their butts to be sniffed and I let them smell mine too. After I have had enough of drawing in air surrounding local dogs, I move along with Bella. I feel like having a personal tour guide and bodyguard on my side.

"Ellie!" Bella calls to the tiny Chihuahua.

"Bella! Great to see you. Who is your new friend?" asks Ellie.

Bella introduces us. She gives her my full name and Ellie understands my title. It is about time. I was starting to feel that Paw Paw School was unknown in this town. Ellie comes from upper-class humans. Her human mom is an important person in town. Everyone knows her.

I have a wonderful time getting to know Ellie and my new friend Bella. Ellie has three wonderful little puppies. I love letting them jump on me. Their tiny sharp claws were fun at the beginning, but I am happy they have now gotten bored and have gone on exploring other places in the park.

While the puppies play, Bella, Ellie, and I have fun chatting. Time just flies by. Ellie's human mom calls to collect the puppies.

"Chloe, Coco, Max! We are leaving!" Chloe and Coco come right away. "Max, C'mon! Where are you?" calls Ellie. But none of us can smell his sweet puppy breath. Ellie starts to run around in a panic.

"Ellie, where is Max?" asks her human mom, picking up Ellie and putting her inside a doggie stroller along with her daughters Chloe and Coco.

Ellie pants in panic. Where is her son Max?

"Maximus, where are you? I am giving a speech about the new homeless shelter in half an hour. I don't have time to look for you!" cries out Ellie's mom in distress.

Max doesn't answer.

Where is he?

"We are going to return later and put up some fliers. I am sorry, Ellie, but we have to go. People know Max; someone will return him to us," she says and turns the stroller away from us while Ellie cries.

"Please help me find him!" Ellie calls at the last moment.

"We will. I promise!" Bella barks back.

This is how Bella got her first case.

3

Mission:

Find Max

"What do you want to do?" I ask Bella when the stroller with Ellie and the pups is out of sight.

"Find Max," she replies calmly. "You can come along or not."

"I am not going to stay long. My mom has to go to work soon."

"I didn't mean now. After our humans leave. Use your doggie door to get in the yard and I can help you get out. Ellie is locked up in her house. She can't get here until the evening. That's too late. We have to help her now. She didn't pay attention to Max because of us."

"You want to return here to the park without our humans?" I ask in disbelief.

"Do you see any other options?" asks Bella.

"But what about the dog catcher?" I ask. I admit I am a little scared. I have never been anywhere without my mom Kathleen.

Not much later, I meet Bella by the fence. She pushes one board in the fence aside and I crawl inside her yard. I am impressed that Bella knows about the loose board in the fence.

"Follow me," Bella says and I do.

I am scared but curious. Bella's yard looks different. They have play structures for the human kids and toys lying in the grass. I'm not sure if these are Bella's or the kids'. It doesn't matter now. My legs are shaking. I am scared to leave my place without a human, but curiosity gets the better of me.

Plus, I want to help poor Ellie. Such a fine lady.

Bella runs along the fence until we reach a bush. She goes behind it and appears on the other side of the fence.

"Hurry up," she huffs, "I dug up a hole there. Nobody will notice."

I hadn't expected that. I don't like to mess up my fur, but at this moment I am all about adventure!

We casually run toward the park, keeping our senses sharp.

"How do you want to get in?" I ask Bella. "There are people. The park is fenced and you need a human . . .". But before I even finish my sen-tence, I see Bella make an enor-mous leap.

She flies up toward the fence where she pushes

herself off the top of the fence with her back paws and jumps to the other side. *Wow.*

"Are you coming?" Bella asks casually.

I look at the top of the fence, calculating the height, and realize that this is higher than any of my maximum jumps in agility class. I am a really good jumper, but I am also smaller than Bella. I simply can't reach the same height as a Husky.

"Maybe I should check around on the outside for some clues," I say. I am a little embarrassed to admit that I may not be able to jump over.

"Good idea. Keep an eye out for the dog catcher. Let's meet here in half an hour," Bella responds. Then she is gone.

I truly admire the way Bella goes with the flow. She faces any situation, acts upon it, and she doesn't get scared or panic. I wonder if she is afraid of anything.

I spend that time sniffing around the park. Too many dog smells. Every tree is covered in hundreds of peemail scents. Trying to find anything left behind by the tiny Chihuahua is close to impossible. All I find is a dead bird that feral cats have scored not too long ago.

"Did you find something?" Bella asks when we meet up again.

"Just a dead bird that cats got recently. You?"

"Interesting. I talked to Zeus, the German Shepherd. He said that he saw Max running toward the fence to watch a cat catch a bird. My instinct says that there is something fishy about it." Bella ponders this.

We go over to the dead bird again to check it out, but it is already gone. Just some feathers left. Bella smells around the place.

"Max could have easily run toward the fence without raising any alert that he was too far away. He is also small enough that there is a chance he made it through the fence." Bella is thinking out loud.

"Don't you think that he would be afraid of an alley cat?" I point out.

"Not Max, he doesn't have enough life experience to make a proper judgment call. He comes from an extremely loving family and has never experienced anything but love and fun," replies Bella.

We spend another hour checking around and then Bella has to return home before her mom and Lucy come back. I don't want to stay out on my own, so I return home too. Kathleen will be home from work soon. I can't say that I enjoy the fact that Max is missing, but I do enjoy having something else to do other than waiting for Kathleen all day in the apartment. It is a challenge to go into the world without Mom. If it weren't for Bella, I wouldn't do it. Maybe it feels that much more exciting because of this. I am starting to like this new place.

When we get home, I stay outside with Bella to chat by the fence. Soon, we see Ellie go by on a leash.

"Did you find Max?" howls Ellie with hope.

"Not yet. No worries, he will be found," Bella encourages her.

"Where are Coco and Chloe?" I ask.

"Mom left them at home. She only took me to call Max. We are bringing flyers and are going to ask around," replies Ellie. "Are you two coming to the park with your moms again today?"

"I never come in the afternoon. Kids are going to be home from school and Mom gets busy. I will come with her in the morning again," replies Bella.

"I don't know yet. My mom used to take me twice a day in our old place, but she said that when we move here I'd have a yard and she won't have to walk me so much," I say truthfully.

A human voice interrupts our conversation.

"C'mon, Ellie, let's go. Don't you want to find Max?" Ellie's mom tugs on her leash.

Humans are not that smart. I understand around two thousand human words and humans seem happy to understand only a few cues like when we wag our tails or stand at the door. Sometimes I wish humans understood us.

"I gotta' go. I'll check with you on my way back," Ellie calls as she runs down the road.

"Poor Ellie," I sigh.

When Kathleen gets home, I act excited to see her and demand my walk. I bounce around and keep running to the door where I stop for a moment.

"Do you like this new place, Gr. Acie?" Kathleen rubs me behind the ears.

Oh, this is heaven.

I wag my tail extra hard. *Mom, are you going to take me to the park?* I try to give her my best puppy eyes. But still nothing. I grab my leash, go to Mom, and then turn to the door.

"I still have so many boxes to unpack, Gr. Acie. Go play in the yard!"

After couple more attempts, I take her advice and sit by the fence. Bella is busy playing with Sofia and Kyle.

I stay by the fence watching Sofia hold a hose with running water and Bella jump and catch the stream of water between her teeth. Lucy is giggling so much she falls on her diaper from seeing such a funny sight.

I have always thought that I am happy it is just me and Kathleen. Especially at night when Kathleen lays in the bed on her side and I crawl up in her lap. Kathleen strokes my fur until we both fall asleep. She often tells me that we girls have to stick together in this world to keep the flame of our inner goddess shining. I am glad I don't have to share Kathleen with anyone.

I lay down and look between the fence boards, watching how active the kids are with Bella and listening to their never-ending giggles. For the first time, I like the idea of having young humans in my pack and the joy it can bring. *No wonder Bella didn't need any canine schooling.* She has no need for agility classes. She has all the training she could need at home with her human family. *What a blessed life we both have.*

Later on, Kathleen meets Bella's Mom, Dad, and her human siblings. Kathleen and Bella's mom agree on taking a walk to the dog park together the next morning! If Kathleen becomes friends with her, Bella and I can spend more time at the park together looking for Max!

4

Need to Explore

I try to wake Kathleen up extra early. She isn't excited about getting up like I am, but she is very loving and makes a bargain to cuddle with me in bed. She kisses my head and pulls me closer to her body.

Bella told me that her humans don't like to get up early either. The smallest human, Lucy, is the only one who likes to get up with Bella. Kyle and Sofia are the complete opposite, almost never willing to get up. We, dogs, like to nap in the day, but we are always ready to get up for adventure.

Later I meet Bella, her mom, and Lucy outside. It is nice to go to the park together. I think that our moms like it too.

When we get to the park, we see flyers for Max on the trees. Ellie is at the park too.

"Any news?" I ask Ellie. Her big eyes look even bigger today. I can feel hope and sorrow in them.

"Nothing yet. Did you hear anything?" asks Ellie.

I want to tell Ellie what Zeus told us, but Bella is faster.

"We are working on it," she says.

"Why didn't you want Ellie to know about Max watching the alley cat?" I ask after Ellie left to go home.

"Because we don't know anything for sure and I don't want to give her false hope," replies Bella. "C'mon, we have a little more time to check this place out."

As soon as she says that, we hear Lucy scream. She has tripped over a branch lying in the grass and scratched her hand. Human puppies apparently can't handle too much. She is wailing loudly.

Bella immediately runs to her side and comforts her. Her human mom runs over too, picks her up, and snuggles her. Our chance to investigate a little more is ruined. Bella's mom decides to take Lucy home. Little Lucy calms down only when she is safely in her mom's arms. Kathleen offers to push the empty stroller back. All of us are returning home sooner than we thought.

With tails between our legs and heads down, we walk home with our humans.

"Are we going out again today?" I ask.

"Why wouldn't we?" Bella replies with a question.

"I wasn't sure if Lucy is going to go to the daycare after the accident. Won't her mom stay at home with her?"

"Look at her. She is already calm. Besides, Mom volunteers at the library today."

I have been to the doggie daycare a few times when Kathleen went on business trips. I didn't mind it, but I didn't like it much either. I was wondering if they put human puppies in kennels there too. Maybe human babies bite each other and the caregivers separate them on walks. I don't want to ask about this. We have a serious problem to solve. We both need to focus on the task for today!

I am excited to get out again. Bella is so fearless! I have never met a dog like her. Although she isn't school educated, she is smart, brave, kind, and even agile. I am really happy we moved to this new place.

When Kathleen goes to work, and Bella's mom takes Lucy to daycare, Bella and I go to work on the case of missing Max.

Today, Bella decides to check the alley where all the feral cats live.

"Are you sure?" I question Bella. "Alley cats are anything but friendly."

"That is where our only clue leads us. You don't have to go if you don't want to. It might not be pretty." Bella shrugs.

"I'm coming."

I don't want to leave Bella alone. Anyway, this is much more fun than sitting on the couch and waiting for my Mom to come home.

5
Alley

I can smell the alley from far away. It's a place for the homeless. Dogs, cats, and even people live there and can be found sleeping outside under the roof of an old abandoned building. Kathleen would never walk me in a place like this. The hair on the top of my back stands up.

There is a small park, if you can call it that, leading up to the building. It is very dirty, full of human trash. The breeze is mixing the aroma of unwashed people and animals. I thought the dog park had a strong signature smell to it, but nothing can beat this place.

I see ravens in the grass trying to mess with empty food containers. A new raven flies in and screeches at his cousins. That sound matches this place. I can't shake off the weird energy of this neighborhood. It is as if some unseen power is squeezing me.

Bella keeps her head low, her nose close to the ground, and her ears lifted. We finally get to the corner of the big old building.

"Well, well, well, looks like we have some fine guests here. What is a pair of salon-groomed ladies like yourselves doing in this neighborhood?" asks a big German Shepherd who appears like a ghost from the other side of the building.

"Thank you." I push back my ears to show the great work of my groomer.

Bella seems ready to talk to him.

"I am Roger," he says. His voice is peaceful. He offers us his behind to smell. Bella sniffs a little into the air to be polite while I look in the other direction. I don't know what to think of a dog who lives *here*. Bella seems to be way more open to conversation.

"I'm Bella and this is Acie," Bella introduces us both.

I was grateful that she didn't use my title. I didn't want to give Roger a chance to laugh at me.

"We are looking for a little Chihuahua puppy. Is there any chance you have smelled, heard, or seen him?" Bella asks.

"No, but I was out with my man all day. I can't smell anything new in this smell factory anyway," replies Roger.

I still didn't think much of him, but for a homeless dog, he seems nice. He spoke of his human as his man, not Dad. I wonder what it is like to sleep on the street and smell the downside of the whole world all the time. I have never spoken to any homeless dogs before.

"My man needs me. You ladies be careful. The alley cats are vicious," Roger says and then disappears.

"Do you think he knows more?" I ask.

"No, he doesn't. He is telling the truth. But he wasn't here at the time Max disappeared either."

"How do you know he is telling the truth?" I ask, still suspicious of him.

"Look who he is," says Bella.

"A homeless dog living with a homeless human that he calls his man?" I can't guess what Bella is thinking.

"A hero. His man is a hero too. Heroes don't lie."

"And you think he is a hero because . . .?"

"He is a pure German Shepherd with manners that lives with a homeless man. He said that his man needed him. Also, he was genuinely concerned about our safety. This dog served in the human army. His Dad is a hero. Many human heroes can't handle the life inside a human kennel after they return from the army. They need their dogs to handle life. I have known other purebred dogs that ended up homeless after serving with their humans in the army, "says Bella, staring ahead.

Then she lowers herself to the ground and moves quietly forward. I duck down and follow in her steps. We pass piles of clothes. Most of the canine and human residents are gone at this time of a day. I can hear cats from the opposite end of this place. *Can they hurt us?* Roger didn't ease my feelings about this place.

"Look at those feathers," Bella points toward the ground.

"These are feathers from the same bird that the alley cat got at the park when Max was last seen!" I exclaim. I took a class on tracking and smell recognition at the Paw Paw School. I can recognize and remember smells well.

I just played a part in this investigation! The unseen power that has been squeezing me loosens up its grip. I feel a little braver and this place is slightly less scary.

Cats hiss and meow in the background. Bella sniffs the feathers and pauses.

"I am close; I know it," Bella assures herself out loud.

"We have to return home now. Our parents will be back soon and will be worried," I point out.

"I know. We will come back tomorrow," sighs Bella.

6
The Afternoon

"Acie! How have you been today?" Kathleen greets me cheerfully when she gets home.

I wag my whole spine, so she knows how happy I am.

"I have a housewarming present for you," Kathleen says, pulling out a stuffed squirrel.

After Kathleen is done with her boring self-grooming routine, we go outside to play with my new toy.

Bella is outside too. Kyle and Sofia are playing with her. I wonder what it is like to have human siblings in the pack. Some of my friends complain about their human brothers or sisters, but Bella just loves the whole family with all her heart.

Kyle takes an apple that Sofia has been eating and gives it to Bella. She accepts it while Sofia squeaks for the apple. Then Sofia starts chasing Bella around the yard. My canine friend folds her ears back and starts running double speed in large circles, holding the apple between her teeth. Lucy is standing in the middle, giggling and clapping her little paws together. The kids bring out a playful side in Bella.

Dogs and human kids can live in the moment. Grown up humans often worry about something that isn't happening now. I am happy I am a dog.

Kathleen throws my new toy squirrel in the grass. I run after it and pretend to make a kill. I pick up the squirrel and shake my neck, growling in my mean voice. Kathleen laughs. I add more growl. I love making Kathleen happy. If she only knew the real adventure I am up to.

I bring the toy back and Kathleen throws it for me a few more times.

When I get tired, I look between the fence boards into Bella's yard. Bella is now lying on her back getting her belly rubbed by the older kids. Lucy's attention turns to me. She wobbles toward the fence and giggles. I wag my tail extra hard and toss my toy squirrel up in the air. I catch it in midair again like a predator catches wild game. Lucy reaches her little hands toward me through the fence.

I bring the toy to the fence and let Lucy toss it for me. She is so excited! Her little hands barely flip the toy up in the air and it

 lands right on my back. I guess you can't expect much of a toss from a human puppy that waddles like a duck and isn't potty trained.

Bella watches Lucy too. Then she gets up, shakes her fur, and comes over to talk to me.

"Interesting," she notes.

"What is?" I ask. I didn't think she would find the primitive toss interesting.

"Lucy found your game interesting, so she came to the fence to be part of it."

"And now she is trying to grab my ear and pull it through the fence. Are you going somewhere with this?" I ask while trying to free my ear from Lucy.

"Think of Lucy as Max, you as a cat, and your toy as a ruse to get Lucy to the fence." Bella hints.

The lightbulb in my head turns on.

7
Clock Is Ticking

The next morning, Bella and I meet Ellie in the park again. She looks like a dog forgotten in the rain. Nobody has called about the flyers. I can't look into her big dark eyes. That much sadness is hard to handle. Coco and Chloe mope around, not even playing like all puppies do. Ellie doesn't take her eyes off her two remaining pups.

"Ellie, we will find your son. Keep your head up!" Bella keeps saying.

"What if he is lost forever? It has been two long nights since he disappeared," whispers Ellie. Her energy is heartbreaking.

No smells could excite her, she isn't willing to play, and she has the saddest puppy eyes ever.

I walk away. It is too much for me. *We need to find Max!* If I wasn't determined enough before, I am now. I sniff around and walk toward the fence where Max was last seen. I decide to look and see if there is a better clue. I sniff around. Too many dogs' smells cover every inch of the dog park.

Bella makes a point of talking to all the dogs in the park. She is quite social. She knows most dogs here and gets along with almost anybody, which is rare. I don't care to know as many dogs, but I was raised differently. Kathleen and I are our own mini-pack. We are two smart girls who love to get our pawdicures done properly. At least this is what Kathleen tells me.

"Did you find out anything?" I ask Bella on our joint walk back from the park.

"Harry, the mutt that snoops around garbage cans, said that he saw a cat carrying away a rat that morning," Bella replies.

I look puzzled. *What did a cat's prey have to do with Max?*

"You saw a dead bird, which soon disappeared. Zeus saw Max running toward the fence to check out the situation. Harry saw a cat carrying a rat away. What do you make of this?" questions Bella. She is heading somewhere with this.

"You think that the rat wasn't really a rat?" I hypothesize.

"Bingo."

"But why would an alley cat eat a puppy? The cat already caught a bird. That just doesn't make sense."

"I think the cat didn't catch it to eat it. Hunger wasn't the motive."

"Then what was it?" I ask.

"I still have to figure that out," replies Bella, absorbed in her thoughts as we return home.

When we get back, I run straight for the couch. I need to take a quick nap before Bella's pack leaves their home for the day. I have a feeling that today won't be easy. Kathleen kisses me goodbye and is off to work.

I dream of hunting squirrels in the trees. I climb the trees and leap from one branch to another. Just when I make my attack and snap for the squirrel, something slaps my face! I open my eyes in an instant. I jump up with a fearless snarl on my face, ready to fight.

Bella is standing by me, wagging her tail.

"Did you ever hear about privacy?" I snap.

"Yeah, my whole human pack, except Lucy, repeats that question all the time to each other, but I guess nobody has gotten the hang of it." Bella laughs.

"How did you get here anyway?"

"You have a doggie door, remember? A bit tight for my size but what wouldn't a Husky do for her Poodle friend," says Bella with a smirk. She is still entertained by my waking up reaction. "Anyway, it's time to go. It's the last day of school and work. We need to solve this today before the weekend comes."

8

Back in

the Alley

The day is darkened by clouds that promise rain. The wind is blowing from the north, which might help us cover our smell tracks. It is as if the weather is expressing the energy of today. Maybe it is the air pressure or maybe the time ticking that is causing me to feel uneasy in my chest.

The alley looks eerie. The wind is blowing old, dirty plastic bags around and spreading the strong aroma of this place far beyond its boundaries. A silhouette of a dog appears in front of us.

"Ladies," Roger greets us.

"Roger." Bella and I sniff the air.

"I was waiting for you," he says.

Bella's ears perk. He knows something.

"What did you find?" Bella cuts straight to the point.

"It was a windy night last night. My man doesn't sleep well during nights like that. I stayed up to make sure he could get some decent sleep," Roger says with deep concern in his voice. "When the moon was the highest, I heard a whining noise coming from the feline residence."

"Cats make all kinds of whining noises," Bella comments.

"This one wasn't from cats," Roger continues with absolute certainty in his voice. "This was a puppy."

"All the clues are leading us here," Bella is thinking out loud, "yet I just can't imagine why cats would kidnap a puppy."

"Could they be using Max for something?" I ask.

"I'm not sure. Let's find out," responds Bella. "I wish we could get close to the cats without being noticed. We need to spy. Is there some way to go inside of this old building and get close to the cats' territory?" she asks Roger.

"Kind of. Long ago this used to be a hotel. There is a way into an old hallway. You could get through there to the other side of the building. But it's dangerous," he replies.

Bella gives him a look of boredom. Danger doesn't faze her.

"The scariest human from this community lives there. He doesn't like other humans, dogs, or cats. If he sees you two, he will try to catch you and wait for your owners to put up flyers for the reward. I have seen him do it a couple of times. He just locks those dogs up in the building. They are lucky if their owners are looking for them fast because he doesn't even feed them," continues Roger.

"Could he be the one who kidnapped Max?" I ask.

"No. He would have responded to the flyers and gotten the reward already," replies Roger.

"Well, he can't catch all of us. I am fast. None of the human kids in my house are ever able to catch me and they try all the time," Bella says with confidence.

"Don't underestimate him. He knows the place and he would easily corner you into one of the many rooms in there and close you in. If you choose to go in, I can't come with you. He knows me. If he sees me there, he would cause problems for my man. I can't put my man in danger."

"I don't want to put you in jeopardy. You have done plenty for us. I am going in," Bella huffs decisively. "You can come with me or not, Gr. Acie. I understand if you don't want to."

What am I supposed to say? I am scared. Knowing that even Roger, one tough

🐾 54

street dog, doesn't want to enter doesn't help. *What if the scary human did get me?* My mom would be so scared. I am her best friend. But I can't leave Bella in that situation alone either.

"I am coming," I say, surprising myself.

When Roger sees that we are determined to go in, he describes the inside of the building for us.

"Try to be as quiet as possible. He is inside now. Your best strategy is not to be seen by him. If he sees you, do not run into any open doors leading into the rooms. Stay in the hallway even if you have to pass by him. That's your only chance. If he traps you into any of the rooms, you have no chance to get out," he warns us.

"I am ready," says Bella.

"Me too," I lie.

9

The Scariest
Moment
of My Life

The hallway has been missing fresh air for ages. It smells of mildew, garbage, and a human who hasn't had a bath for a very long time. A long line of windows provides plenty of light despite the fact that they are filthy. Opposite the windows is a wall with many open doors. These must be the rooms Roger was telling us about. Crumbled papers from fast food places, empty bottles, and cans are randomly lying around on the floor.

Bella and I don't say a word to each other. We have a plan. We must get from one side of the hallway to the other, turn the corner, and make it to the other end of the building where the cats live. The bad human has taken up residence in the corner room. This gives him the chance to see what is happening on both ends of the place. It's a strategic position for him and unfortunate for us.

Bella drops her head and tail down and starts to place one paw in front of the other. Her body reminds me of coyotes on the hunt. She is quiet, slow, and careful. I wait for her to get a little distance from me before I start crouching in the same way behind her.

The floor is made of tiles. It is hard to keep our claws from scraping against them and not making noise. We don't want to make any sounds. Suddenly, a mouse runs in front of us. Under any other circumstance, I would start chasing it, but in this situation, it doesn't trigger my instincts. Bella stops for a moment.

The mouse runs off. My heart is racing. I feel like I am part of something monumental.

When Bella reaches the corner of the hallway, she stops and sniffs the air. She is outside of the mean human's room. The doors to all the rooms are open, including his. Bella lies down on the floor and sticks her nose into the doorway. Carefully, she crawls past the door. *She made it!*

My best friend turns around and gives me the look to proceed with caution. I can smell my own fear. *Get it together Acie*, I tell myself. It takes all I have to follow Bella who is waiting, ready to attack the man if needed. Having a pal like her gives me the confidence to keep going. I try to pull my claws in like a cat. Then, I slowly crawl past the doorway facing forward, too scared to look into the room. *I made it!*

The second part of the hallway is darker due to the trees and shrubs growing just outside of the windows that are blocking the light. Just like in the first part there are open doors into rooms opposite the windows. We hear some meows from outside. The sound is clear, which means there must be an opening into the cat's territory. I get a whiff of fresh air.

We are lucky. When we get to the end of the hallway to check out the situation, there is a narrow window and we find a small hole in the corner of the floor. Based on the hole's size, rats must have dug it to create an escape route for themselves.

We both lie down with our noses toward the opening. This may take a while. If the mean man sees us here, we will be in trouble. This is a place that we could get trapped in easily.

I smell so many strong smells. Trying to catch the smell of a puppy is close to impossible. But Bella isn't giving up. She is lying down and waiting like a wild predator waiting for its prey. Just when I am about to give up, we hear a tiny whimper. Our ears perk up. I exchange a look with Bella. Yes, this is a little puppy indeed.

We hear some cats and then we hear the whimper again. Bella stands up slowly and silently straightens herself on her back paws, placing her front paws on the ledge of the window. She lowers her head and watches the alley outside. I am curious to know what she sees, but I know it would be too much risk to do the same so I keep smelling and listening by the hole.

We hear another whine from a puppy. *Is that Max?* I look up at Bella. She is laser focused on something in the alley. Quietly, she lowers herself back down to the ground, looks at me, and turns around. She knows something! I stand up from my position and we both start to go back.

Maybe it is because we are in a hurry or maybe our claws hit the floor too hard, but we run into trouble ourselves.

Just when Bella passes the corner, the mean human storms out. I am behind her, which puts him right in between us.

He must be one of the biggest humans I have ever seen. His legs are monstrous. He is wearing a pair of ripped old pants that are carrying many different smells and shades. His shoes are much newer but are still covered in mud. He stomps in my direction. I am scared to look up. His legs alone seem like the scariest things I have ever seen.

Oh no. This isn't good! I am trapped in the part of the hallway that has no escape to the outside!

The fur on my back stands up straight as soon as I lift my head. Time has frozen for a moment. I am looking at a huge body wearing multiple layers of shirts and something that was a jacket at one point a long time ago. He opens up his arms as if he wants to give someone a hug, and out of the long sleeves come hands that are as big as Bella's head. He is coming for me!

I dare to look even higher at his head. His glowing eyes hypnotize me. Bushy eyebrows surround his eyes, with a big nose in the middle. He has curly fur on his face but is missing fur on the top of his head. Instead, he has darker spots there that look like the skin of a cheetah. He looks almost like an animal himself.

Finally, he chuckles. "Look at this. I didn't even expect this to be my lucky day! Come here, doggie. I bet your owners love you like their own child."

I panic and turn back to the cat's corner and start running.

"Acie, you need to turn to him and run my way!" Bella barks intensely. "There is no escape! You need to pass him!"

I know that too, but my legs are running instinctively away from him. I have no control over my body. *What is he going to do to me?*

The mean human lets out something like a laugh and marches toward me. He isn't running. He knows I have nowhere to run so it won't be hard to catch me. He marches with his big arms spread, pushing me further into the corner where I was listening to cats just a minute ago.

"You gotta' turn around, Acie!" I hear Bella urge.

I am turning my head to the man, but my paws are leading me away from him and into the trap. I am terrified.

I reach the corner. The man laughs. The only place to go is an open door that leads into a room. I start backing up.

"Noooooo," howls Bella.

"I'm sorry," I whimper back.

Then all of a sudden, there is Bella. She attacks the man from behind and bites one of his arms. This finally shakes me up. I run under his legs and keep going. The world becomes one big blur. Thankfully, I hear Bella running behind me. We both make it.

10

Cat Fight

"What's the rush?" Roger laughs when he sees us dash out of the place.

We run into some nearby bushes. Roger follows us there.

"I'm guessing you woke up Bob," he says, still laughing.

"Why are you laughing? We could have been murdered!" I bark back at him.

"But you weren't," he points out.

"Hey, you two, let's not forget why we are here," Bella interrupts.

"What did you find out?" asks Roger.

We tell him about the whining sound we heard.

"I think I know where they are keeping Max," says Bella. "After the whine, I saw a big tomcat with a torn ear that jumped up on the garbage can and hissed."

"Makes sense. That was Tom; he is the feline leader," explains Roger.

"That would be an easy place to keep puppies trapped," I conclude.

"Roger! Roger!" We hear a human call.

"That's my man. I have to go. Are you going to be okay on your own now?" asks Roger.

"Go to your human," says Bella. "You did a lot for us. Thank you!"

Roger wags his tail goodbye and leaves.

With adrenaline still pumping in our blood, we both cheer, "Let's go get Max!"

We pretend that we wandered to this side of the alley where cats live, by accident. Sniffing through the grass, we start to get close to the suspicious garbage can. The only way to blend into this environment is to stand out. It is obvious neither one of us belongs here. But I am no longer scared. There is excitement pumping in my blood from surviving the scariest moment of my life. I feel like the world's best secret agent. I smell feline markings and coughed up hairballs. I will never understand why some humans prefer cats over dogs. These creatures are so . . .

"Tsssk-tsssk!" I hear above my head. Bella and I look up and see a calico cat.

The game is on!

"You don't belong here," hisses the cat.

Bella looks up and growls quietly. "Tell me something I don't know."

I hold back the urge to bark. We don't need all of the cats here. The garbage can is still out of our reach. Cats could take the puppy away before we could get to him. We need to get another fifty yards closer.

"Two lost canine souls," meows the calico cat out loud.

"Do you have nothing better to do than meow all over the alley?" asks Bella.

"But I do it so well!" cries the calico cat. "Look! You are about to be welcomed by my friends!"

She is right. Suddenly there are cats coming toward us from every angle.

Bella rolls her eyes. We run into the gabbiest cat in the alley.

I look at Bella. *I got this. You sneak away and save Max!* I signal her by giving a quick look toward the garbage can.

I start barking and barking at all the cats that are slowly closing in on me while Bella quietly backs up toward the suspicious trash can. I am holding back my urge to jump at them, but I need to look powerless and let them make fun of me to keep them distracted. Nothing in the world works better than feeding their swollen-headed vain characters. Cats love to have the upper hand over dogs. Thankfully, they aren't as smart as us and I am using that to my advantage. I am proud of myself for not being afraid.

I am barking in a high-pitched voice and panting like a dog gone mad in between my barks. I wag my tail and even stand up on my hind legs for a moment.

I am surrounded by about a dozen cats that are having the time of their life.

"This is really good," meows one cat, choking from her laugh.

"Best show this month!" A black cat awards my performance as she almost falls off the tree she is watching me from.

Meanwhile, Bella gets all the way to the trash can. She has a pretty clear path toward victory. She sneaks up to the can, stands up on her back legs, places her paws on the top, and pushes her nose into the lid to pop it open.

Snap! The lid comes off. Bella looks inside.

I am trying to see what is happening. But instead, I see the leader cat Tom crawl onto the branch of a tree just above Bella.

Plop! I watch him jump right onto Bella's neck. Sharp claws pierce her skin. She drops down on all her four legs, turns her head back, and sees Tom, the big gray tomcat with a torn ear. She spins around furiously, trying to shake him off. *If only she could reach behind her neck to bite him!* She looks enraged. And so does Tom.

Tom's fur is standing straight, his yellow eyes are wide open and his mouth is hissing like a hundred snakes put together. Bella knows that she needs to take care of him fast before the other cats notice what is really going on. I wish cat's hearing was as bad as humans', but unfortunately, they can hear as well as canines.

I am trying to distract all the cats. But at the same time, I am distracted by peeking in the direction of Bella.

"Woof, woof, woof," I carry on.

Meanwhile, Bella jumps on top of the garbage can and then immediately jumps off. The garbage can falls on its side and the impact of hitting the ground with her front paws throws Tom right onto the pavement face first. It distracts me from barking. I am curious to know what's happening.

"I guess cats do have nine lives." Bella finally laughs.

The fight is not over, and she knows it, but this is a small victory.

"Meeeoooww," cries Tom.

The loud meow wakes me up from the spell I have felt like I was under. I realize I was quiet for a second, which isn't good. Who would guess that just a split second of silence would make all the cats turn their heads toward what was really happening?

"We've been tricked!" the cats meow and immediately start running toward Tom. I run with them.

Bella and Tom stick their heads inside the trash can and I hear a yelp. I see Tom pull out a little puppy. But he doesn't have a hold on him for too long. Bella places her jaws around Tom's neck and growls furiously. Tom spits out that little dude. Bella grabs the puppy.

I reach Bella who is now getting attacked by cats. She looks at me and signals for me to run. Striking cats fall off Bella's big husky body as soon as she vaults out of here. We rush out and don't stop until we reach the street and there are no longer any cats behind us.

My heart is pounding when we finally stop in the bushes nearby. Bella lets the pup down on the ground. I am finally sure that this is Max.

"Are you alright?" Bella asks Max.

"I th . . . th . . . think so." Max shudders.

"Do you remember us, Max?" Bella asks softly.

"You are my mom's friends, right? Will you take me home?" Max asks politely.

"Of course, puppy breath. Your mom has been worried about you. Your whole pack has been searching for you. They will be happy to have you back," says Bella.

I lick his big eyes and clean his face. This bit of motherly care returns the sparkle to his eyes.

"Do you know why the cats took me?" asks Max.

"Yes, I do," Bella replies to my surprise. "But let's tell you on our way back. We all need to get home quickly now. Are you strong enough to run on your own? I bet you are starving."

"I will run on my own to my family!" exclaims Max. "I am very hungry. The cats only gave me water to drink, but I can't wait to see my pack."

We start trotting back.

"Here, look at this poster," Bella points out the poster that is near the old hotel building.

"Making our town a better place for everyone," I read out loud. "It's catchy, I guess, but what does it have to do with Max?" I ask.

"Keep reading," says Bella.

"A homeless shelter with a clean park coming soon," I read further. There is a drawn picture of that old hotel, but it looks nice with a clean park and blooming flowers around it. In front of this picture is the smiling face of Max's human mom! I feel even more confused than before.

"Max's mom is in charge of this project. Humans in our town are going to renovate that old hotel and turn it into a place for all the homeless people in this town. Part of the project is to clean up the small park around the hotel. That is where all the feral cats live. All these cats are supposed to be caught and put into feline foster care.

"Tom and his gang didn't want to lose their feral lifestyle. They planned to trap Max and let him starve for a few days. When Tom jumped on my neck, he told me that I was wasting my time trying to return Max. Tom hissed that he was going to let the mean human from the hotel return Max for the reward.

"Then it all made sense to me. The cats had hoped that Max's human mom would stop the project if the mean man from the hotel brought her starving puppy home and demanded money. She would get upset at all the homeless people and the cats wouldn't be caught and put into the care of humans," explains Bella.

11

Home
Sweet Home

I have never been this happy to return home before.

Kyle and Sofia meet us at the end of our street with glee. They have been worried and looking for Bella. We are heroes for bringing the little puppy home!

Bella's mom is relieved and happy to see her dog come home safely. She is excited to see Max and me too. She lifts me over the fence and into my yard, wags her finger in the air, and tells me to wait for my mom there. Then, she calls Ellie's mom to tell her the good news.

I take a well-deserved dognap in my yard. I wake up hearing the doorbell to Bella's house. It's Ellie with her two pups in the stroller and both of her human parents. She can hardly be contained inside. Bella's mom opens the door with Max in her arms. Ellie squeaks with happiness. She is scratching the stroller, barking and wagging her tail to get out. Bella's mom encourages Ellie's parents to let them all meet and play in the yard, but first she hands Max to his humans. They take him, hug and kiss him, and put him down to be welcomed by anxious Ellie and his siblings who burst out of the stroller as soon as it opens. Max jumps on his mom while Chloe and Coco leap onto Max. They look like a ball of joy. They are rolling around licking and greeting each other. Both of their humans squat and pet them all. Then they get up and ask for Bella. When Bella comes outside, Ellie's humans pet her and thank her.

I feel full of joy myself to see such a sight.

"Thank you, Bella," says Ellie heartfully.

"My pleasure," responds Bella and looks in my direction. "I couldn't have done it without Gr. Acie."

Ellie runs to the fence toward me and her humans follow her.

"Thank you! Thank you!" she shouts happily.

"Thank you, Gracie!" call her humans.

I don't mind that they are messing up my name. I am grateful to be part of this moment. I look between the fence boards at Bella. She is smiling at me. What a moment!

After the humans finish chatting, they all leave. Bella and I lie down against each other with the fence in the middle. We don't say a word. We just share the glowing energy between us.

When Kathleen returns home, she doesn't know if she should be upset with me for being gone, or proud of me for returning with Max. In the end, she decides to snuggle me real close that night because she never wants to lose me.

I enjoy the closeness of her body, but I can't sleep from all the adventures I have experienced in just a few days of living here. I think I am going to love this new home. Something tells me that this is just the beginning!

Dictionary

word	meaning
feral	an animal that escaped from a home and became wild
ponder	think about very carefully
sorrow	deep sadness
hypothesize	suggest an explanation to a problem
eerie	mysterious and frightening

alley	a narrow passage between buildings or trees
conclude	to form an opinion after a research or thought
adrenaline	a substance that body creates when someone is feeling a strong emotion, that gives the person more energy
showdown	a final argument, fight or game
feline	related to the cats
canine	related to the dogs

Sneak Peek of

Detective Bella Unleashed

Book 2

1

I love these sunny days. I am lying like a dead dog in the backyard, letting the sun heat my fur. Bella is doing the same in her yard. Sunbathing is one of the few things that I can do for longer than Bella. My light-colored fur allows me to enjoy this warm, fuzzy feeling longer than she can. Bella's dark fur, on the other paw, warms up too fast. I bet she can be outside in the winter when I like to lie down by the fireplace, though.

My eyes are closed, but since I'm a dog, my hearing is still sharp. I hear the back door at Bella's house open, and then I hear Kyle, her human thirteen-year-old brother, step outside. I don't need to open my eyes to know that. I can hear Kyle's typical young-boy walk. I wouldn't pay much attention to the sound normally, but this time, I sense that he is moping. I hear a sigh.

I open my eyes, lift my head, and look over the fence into Bella's yard. Something is not right. Kyle is usually a happy boy who goes with the flow. Now he looks gloomy. He drags his feet over to Bella who sits up when she sees him. Kyle squats down and Bella licks his face in a motherly way. These warm, wet kisses melts Kyle's emotions. He embraces Bella, presses his head into her fur, and starts sobbing.

Bella patiently soaks up his sorrow and lets him take a minute to release the pain from his heart.

Humans need that. I think that is the reason they say we are man's best friend. Humans need someone who is always there for them and just listens. When our humans are sad, we offer our bodies to be hugged or petted, which makes them feel safe. It's quite simple and effective. I don't understand why so many humans can't figure this out for themselves. They hug each other in joy, but often forget that a sad human needs a hug even more than a happy one. Maybe it's the lack of fur on humans. They probably like to insert their paws into our fur because petting us makes them feel better. It works for us too because we love to be pampered.

"I didn't do it, Bella." Kyle weeps into her fur. "I know you believe me, but I'm afraid you're the only one." Kyle starts to calm down as he continues to stroke Bella's fur.

Turning away from this heartbreaking scene, I walk up onto my porch and lie down. I feel bad for Kyle. I mean, he may be a thirteen-year-old human who still acts like a puppy, but he is a good boy. Often, I see him toss his little sister Lucy into the air and when he catches her, she giggles and screams, "More! More!" Just yesterday he was crawling in their yard letting Lucy ride his back as if he were a horse. He made her feel empowered. Sometimes he playfully teases his other sister, Sofia, and she teases him back. They are like two puppies who love to play tug-of-war. Seeing him fall apart and shattered like this isn't normal. Something is very wrong.

"Everyone thinks I did it. I can't blame them because it really looks like I did." Kyle confides in Bella loudly enough for me to hear. Then he buries his head in her fur again and whispers into her ear.

Kyle stays with Bella for quite a while longer, until he is calm and his mom calls him to come inside.

When Kyle goes inside, Bella gets up, and paces over to the fence. She prowls back and forth by the fence. I get up and meet her there. She looks furious. I don't know how to ask what is going on with Kyle. If Bella weren't my friend I'd be afraid to approach her. *Did somebody harm Kyle?* Bella is walking the way dogs do when one of their pack members gets attacked. I greet her by smelling the air near her head.

"I think I have another case to solve," says Bella sharply. "Do you want to help?"

"Of course. Anything for my Husky friend and her human brother," I reply with certainty.

"Kyle is in big trouble. Grownups accused him of something bad, but I know he didn't do it. We need to find the real villain," huffs Bella.

"I know you can do that," I encourage her.

"It will take work," says Bella, "but I believe I can find the culprit. Getting humans to understand me will be the real challenge."

I agree. Getting a dog's point across to a human is like catching a squirrel. You can try with all your might, but you rarely succeed.

"What do you think really happened?"

Be the first to know what happens next!

To get Gr. Acie's FREE book, "A Dog's Guide to Humans", please go to:

http://bit.ly/dogsguide

In addition to giving you Gr. Acie's guide for free, I'll be sure to let you know as soon as the next adventure book is ready. AND, you'll get the new book for a special discounted rate.

If you enjoyed this book, please go to Amazon and post a review.

Thank you!

Acknowledgements

There were many people and dogs who supported me on the journey of writing this book.

Thank you all from the bottom of my heart for helping me to write and continually improve this book.

Special thanks to **Minette Wasserman** for the beautiful illustrations and the patience she had to work with me,

Kristin George for her editing job and her insight into children's book writing,

Rebecca Cuevas for editing, proofreading and above all, for being there for me every step of the way through another publishing journey.

And of course, my gratitude goes to my spectacular launch team.

Thank you.

About the Author

Otakara grew up consuming books like candies. Ever since she was a child, she has wanted to become an author and write books for kids.

She loved animals more than any of her friends did, and often drove her parents crazy with all the living creatures she brought home.

Finally, when she was twelve years old she got a dog named Jessi, and her life was forever changed by the canine love.

Detective Bella Unleashed series grew out of her life spent with dogs by her side, putting words into their mouths and commenting on life from their point of view.

Currently she lives in the beautiful Cascade mountain range in Oregon. She enjoys raising five dogs as well as many other pets, and going on road trips with her homeschooled daughter.

Made in the USA
San Bernardino, CA
04 August 2018